A BELL FOR RINGELBLUME

TO RUTH

Other Books by Rosalie K. Fry

BANDY BOY'S TREASURE ISLAND
BUMBLEBUZZ
CINDERELLA'S MOUSE AND OTHER FAIRY TALES
LADYBUG! LADYBUG!
PIPKIN SEES THE WORLD
THE WIND CALL

A BELL FOR
RINGELBLUME

Written and illustrated by
ROSALIE K. FRY

E. P. DUTTON & COMPANY, INC.
NEW YORK, 1957

Library of Congress Catalog Card Number: 57-5337

Chapter One

"Wake up, Sleeping Beauty!"

Lucinda knew it was Daddy's voice and she knew he was speaking to her, and yet when she opened her eyes she wondered if she was still dreaming, for she seemed to have wakened in a land of make-believe. It's true she was still aboard the train on which they had traveled all day, but the countryside they were passing came straight out of her fairy-tale book at home. While she slept, the hills had grown into great mountains with a glitter of snow on the highest peaks and on the lower slopes, mysterious forests where anything might happen. A waterfall streamed from a high ledge far

5

above the forest, but it turned to a mist of wind-blown spray before it reached the trees.

"Well, what do you think of the Austrian Tirol?" asked Daddy. "Are the mountains as high as you expected?"

"I didn't know mountains could be as high as these," said Lucinda. "And how do you suppose anyone ever climbs up there?" She pointed to a little brown hut in a steep green field above the waterfall.

Mommy leaned across from the opposite seat. "Well one thing is very certain," she said, "you won't need to do much pretending here, because you'll be living all day in a fairyland come true!"

Lucinda was eight-and-a-quarter and she was always ready for any sort of magic that might come her way. Both her parents were artists, and she was accustomed to wandering off and amusing herself while they painted. And as this always happened in some very lovely place, it was usually surprisingly easy to pretend.

But there was no time for dreaming now; the train began to slow down and the carriage was full of sudden bustle as everybody got up and began taking luggage down from the racks.

"This is where we change trains for the last little bit up the valley," Daddy said, as he lifted her down from the high train on to the railway tracks—there was no platform on this side of the line but nobody seemed to worry.

When Lucinda saw the funny little train that was waiting to take them up the valley, she wondered again if she were

6

still asleep. It was exactly like a toy train with its stumpy little engine and tiny wooden coaches. But Daddy seemed to think it was meant to be used and was already piling luggage onto an open platform at the end of one of the cars. So Lucinda climbed in and sat on the wooden seat beside Mommy, waiting to see what would happen next.

When everyone was settled, the engine gave a gay little chirruping whistle—whee-oooo-ee—and began to move. And now Lucinda was quite sure that it really must be a toy train come to life to take them all into an enchanted country. For surely no grown-up human world could possibly look like this!

On both sides of the tracks were the prettiest little houses—*chalets*, Mommy called them. Some were white and some were brown and nearly all had carved wooden balconies,

7

bright with flowers of every color, scarlet, crimson, white, blue, and yellow. Lucinda had time to see them all as the train chugged slowly by. There were carvings, too, and paint-

ings on many of the whitewashed walls. She had a glimpse of a cherub on a cloud and several saints and angels, and a surprising picture of a peasant girl standing in the middle of a wheatfield, throwing her sickle into the air. She wanted to point this out to Daddy and ask him what it meant, but

already the scene was hidden behind another painted chalet.

Perhaps most exciting of all was the river which raced along by the railway line, tumbling over itself in little foaming eddies in its hurry. Never in her life had Lucinda seen such wonderfully colored water. It wasn't quite blue and it wasn't quite green. It reminded her of the aquamarine in Mommy's ring.

"Can I stand outside on the platform with the luggage?" she asked.

"Yes, as long as you're sensible," said Mommy.

As the train made its slow way up the valley they seemed

to be climbing into the clouds. Great fluffy bands of soft cloud-mist lay along the sides of the mountains, which rose out of the haze like a world of make-believe. Lucinda looked up to the highest cloud of all and as she watched, a break appeared like a window in the whiteness. But instead of the blue sky she expected to see, she had a glimpse of cows in a sunny mountain pasture high above the clouds.

Presently the train drew into a miniature station. And there, standing on the platform was the oddest little figure that Lucinda had ever seen. He was exactly like one of the hunchbacked gnomes in her oldest fairy-tale book. He wore a long gray cape with a pointed hood and the heaviest boots and the thickest socks she had ever seen in her life. He was not much taller than she was and he stooped as he stumped toward the train. As he passed below her, Lucinda saw that his rough gray cape was beaded with mist as though he had come from the clouds. She slipped into the carriage and sat beside her mother.

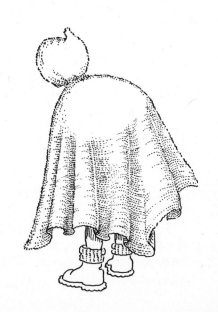

"Hullo!" said Mommy. "Tired of standing out there?"

Lucinda didn't answer. She was too busy watching the gnome as he struggled awkwardly up the steps of the train and stood on the platform on the very spot where she had just been standing. She edged closer to her mother and slipped a hand in hers.

And then the gnome threw back his hood and Lucinda was astonished to see that instead of white hair and a long white beard, he had the head of an ordinary little boy! Then he took off his wet gray cape and she saw that the hump on his back was only a heavy knapsack, which he now swung off his shoulders and dumped on the floor at his feet. Then, taking an apple out of his pocket, he leaned on the rail and settled down to enjoy the journey.

Lucinda let go of Mommy's hand but she did not return to the platform. She couldn't help feeling that a boy who wore a cape like that might really be some sort of gnome from the mountains above the clouds.

Soon it began to get dark and lights appeared in the chalet windows, sending bright shafts streaming over the flowers in the window boxes. And far away up the mountainside in little homes small lights twinkled and shone like stars in the sky.

By the time they reached their destination, it was quite dark and Lucinda had only a confused impression of a village street with flowers in the lighted windows and a burst of song from an open doorway, and somewhere beyond it all the roar of the rushing river. They crossed a narrow bridge which swayed under them as they walked. It was too dark to see the river but they heard it roaring close beneath their feet. Lucinda clung to her father's hand and stumbled along, too tired to care about anything, until suddenly right in front of them was another chalet with lighted windows.

"Here we are!" cried Daddy, who had stayed there many times before. The chalet door flew open as he spoke, and it seemed to the sleepy Lucinda that crowds of people came pouring out to greet them in a language she couldn't understand. She fancied she saw the gnome-boy there and a little girl with a baby, but perhaps it was only part of a dream. She only knew she was taken upstairs and bundled into a big soft bed, where she had one last drowsy glimpse of Mommy, who seemed to be covering her with a cloud as she fell asleep.

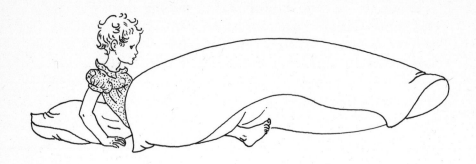

Chapter Two

Lucinda woke to find herself half-buried under the great white mound she had mistaken for a cloud the night before. It was the funniest thing she had ever seen on a bed, twice as fat as an eiderdown and six times as big as a pillow and nothing to tuck in anywhere!

She sat up and looked about the little room she had been too tired to notice when she went to bed. It had plain brown wooden walls and a plain brown wooden ceiling, but the boards of the floor had been scrubbed until they were white and thin white curtains fluttered in the open window. Suddenly she saw that the window opened onto a balcony. The feather-filled "cloud" flew onto the floor as she jumped out of bed to explore.

14

It was the loveliest little balcony, just the right size for one, with a carved wooden balustrade, on top of which stood fifteen flowerpots in a row, with flowers in every one. There were red and white geraniums and pink carnations hanging down in long festoons like party decorations. There were glossy, thick begonias, some yellow and some orange, and a pot of gay petunias with deep purple trumpets.

Suddenly there was a sound of bells, tink-tonk-tinkle-tonk, ringing out in the clear morning air. Lucinda peered between the geraniums and she saw three cows coming slowly down the hillside. They were smaller than the cows at home and very pretty, with soft brown faces and fluffy ears. Around their necks, on leather collars, hung sweet-toned bells which tinkled as they moved. When they came near she saw that they were being driven by the gnome-boy from the train. He wore leather shorts today with funny suspenders, and he looked about twelve years old. But Lucinda remembered his misted hood and was careful not to be seen in case he was really a gnome, driving a fairy herd down from the mountains above the clouds. There was no doubt about it, those bells sounded just like fairy music.

But now she heard another sound, the clink of cups and saucers, and she realized that something was happening next door. For the first time she noticed a tall door at the end of her balcony. She pushed it open, and there on a balcony just like her own sat Mommy and Daddy with a table between them laid for three.

"Ah, there you are darling!" said Mommy. "Hungry?"

"Starving," said Lucinda. "Are we going to have breakfast out here?"

"We are," said Mommy. "So get dressed quickly. Here's a can of water. Take it along and wash properly, won't you? Careful dear, don't spill it!"

It really wasn't possible to wash very much with the

thought of breakfast on the balcony, so Lucinda was soon dressed. As she pulled up her chair to the table, a little girl appeared with breakfast on a tray.

"Guten Morgen," she said shyly, smiling at Lucinda.

"Guten Morgen," Mommy and Daddy answered.

The little girl looked no more than eleven and yet to Lucinda's amazement she wore real earrings, silver ones with little swinging bobbles, while her hair was braided up into a crown, as though she were really a grownup. But perhaps in this strange country anything was possible for the little girl's dress came straight out of a picture book, with its brightly embroidered red bodice and blue and white apron over a full black skirt.

"What did you say to each other?" Lucinda asked when the little girl had gone.

"Guten Morgen—that's German for good morning," explained Daddy.

Breakfast was delicious, crisp white rolls with cherry jam and lovely creamy butter in long curly twists.

Just as they finished their meal, there came a sound of voices below. Lucinda ran to the edge of the balcony and looked over. There was the little girl again, carrying a nice fat baby with fluffy yellow hair. Behind her came a younger sister. Lucinda noticed that she wore earrings, too, shaped like tiny blue forget-me-nots, and around her neck a white bone flower hung on a thin black ribbon. She was carrying a wooden tub which she put on a sunny patch of grass under an apple tree. She then poured a bucketful of water into it, and between them they undressed the baby and lifted her into the tub. She looked even fatter without her clothes, as she sat splashing in the water.

The two little girls soaped her carefully all over, then their stout, smiling mother came out to dry and dress the baby and brush her hair into a long fat sausage on top of her head. Then she emptied the tub and went indoors, leaving the children under the trees.

"Oh, may I go down and play with them?" begged Lucinda.

"You may not find it so easy to play," remarked Daddy. "They can't speak a word of English you know."

"Well anyway I can say 'Guten Morgen' to them!" laughed Lucinda, racing off.

But after they had all said "Guten Morgen" twice, there didn't seem to be anything else to say. When Lucinda asked, "Can I play with you?" they only giggled shyly and said, "Bitte?" which didn't really help.

It was the baby who helped unexpectedly by suddenly getting to her feet and staggering across the grass. In the excitement that followed, Lucinda quite forgot that she didn't speak the language, it was so easy to understand that the baby had never walked before and that her name was Lisbet. The other two were Annali and Gretchen, and by counting on their fingers they explained that Annali was eleven and Gretchen nine. Soon a three-year-old brother came out of the house and joined them. He wore diminutive leather shorts laced up the sides of his little legs, which were even fatter than Lisbet's. His name was Ludwig.

Before long they were all playing house, and Lucinda discovered that you don't need to know the language to play house in another country. They made a cosy bed for Lisbet in the empty tub, only she would keep scrambling out, which was rather tiresome. They used a bench from the porch as a table on which they chopped up different colored flowers and made them into salads, which they arranged artistically on flat leaf-plates. In the middle of the table stood half a broken

flowerpot filled with tiny wind-fall apples. Ludwig insisted on tasting the salads which made his sisters very angry. But nobody seemed to mind how many apples he ate, although they were green and very hard.

From time to time Annali or Gretchen was called away to help with some job in the house, but the game went on happily under the trees in spite of interruptions, and Lucinda was astonished when her mother called from the balcony that it was time for lunch.

Chapter Three

Lucinda had hoped to be able to play with Annali and Gretchen again after lunch, but she found that their mother had work for them indoors. So she was glad when her parents got out their painting things, for she knew that she would be free to wander about and do some exploring while they painted.

Daddy settled down on the river bank.

"Although how I am ever going to get the milky look of that marvelous blue-green water I do not know," he remarked, as he set up his easel.

Mommy found it harder to settle, but at last she found what she wanted, a wide flowery meadow sloping up into the woods.

"Do put these into your picture," said Lucinda, bending over a clump of frail blue flowers like wide-eyed upturned harebells. "If you look at them quickly enough they almost seem to be lit up like little lamps."

"You're quite right," said Mommy. "They do! Indeed the whole field looks rather like a wide green sky scattered with gleaming blue stars."

"Oh, Mommy, that's just exactly what it does look like!" declared Lucinda delightedly. "Oh and look! Here's a little path through the grass. Good-by, I'm going to start my exploring by walking across the green sky!"

"Don't go too far," warned Mommy, unfolding her sketching stool.

As Lucinda followed the little path, the flowers grew taller about her until she was shoulder-high in Queen Anne's Lace and buttercups. Suddenly she was surprised to hear a peculiar clickety noise and something flew over her head on whirring, flame-colored wings and disappeared into the grass. But when she darted after it, she was disappointed to find nothing but a large grasshopper without any sign of wings. She was turning away to look somewhere else, when the grasshopper made a sudden leap into the air and there were the flame-colored wings again, whirring toward the woods. As she moved, another rose up from under her feet and flew after the first on shining blue-green wings.

"Oh how beautiful!" exclaimed Lucinda. "They surely must be messengers sent to lead me into the Enchanted Wood!" And immediately she was deep in a fairy tale.

The wood was certainly just like fairyland. In places the firs and larches grew far apart and the mossy ground was carpeted with flowers. Some she had seen in gardens and some in pictures, but few of them growing wild like this and never in a wood. She tip-toed silently through the trees, pretending she was a lost princess in the heart of a magic forest.

Suddenly a beautiful speckled deer darted across her path. He stopped for a moment to stare at her with large gentle eyes, then bounded away out of sight.

"Oh he must have been Little Brother!" she thought, remembering the well-loved story of Little Brother and Little Sister.

A moment later she came face to face with a monster snail in a queer pale shell. She stopped in surprise, wondering if the snail was as big as it seemed, or if she herself was growing small, like Alice in Wonderland. Suddenly she felt that

the wood was becoming a bit too enchanted for her liking, and it was a comfort to look back and see her parents still painting in the valley below. Then Mommy looked up and waved to her and everything suddenly seemed all right after all. Avoiding the snail she turned back into the sunny wood and her world of make-believe.

She was not at all surprised when she came upon a little

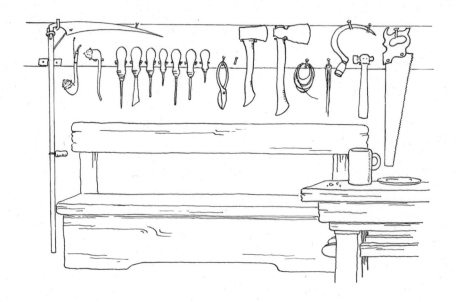

brown hut in a clearing between the trees. It could well be part of any fairy story. The porch was untidy in a comfortable sort of way and full of all sorts of fascinating things. Unfortunately the wide roof of the porch cast so deep a shadow that it was hard to see all that was there. She was able to make out a shining scythe and a great number of tools hanging along the wall and a wonderful curly pipe with a little silver cover. The long table was littered with crumbs, and a plate and mug had been pushed to one side as though someone had eaten a hurried meal and not yet cleared it away. And yet the door was shut and the whole place had a deserted air.

Perhaps, thought Lucinda with a sudden little shiver of excitement mixed with uneasiness, perhaps it's under a spell like the Sleeping Beauty's palace—only it's more like a woodcutter's hut than a palace.

There was a sound of running water behind the hut, and as nobody seemed to be about she went cautiously around to explore. And there she found the most surprising thing in the whole of the Enchanted Wood. Standing on the pedestal of a wooden pump was the figure of a beautiful little peasant girl, carved in wood and delicately painted. She wore a long blue dress with a black, laced bodice and her pale gold hair was braided around her head. In her hand she carried a sickle with a silver-painted blade. As the leaf-shadows trembled across her, she almost seemed alive and Lucinda whispered to herself, "She must be the woodcutter's beautiful daughter turned into wood by some spell."

Lucinda picked a bunch of small pale-yellow foxgloves and put them into the peasant girl's arms to comfort her, before tip-toeing away.

25

She was wandering slowly back through the wood when she came upon a spray of the bluest flowers she had ever seen, big blue trumpets growing in pairs along a curving stem. Just as she was stooping down to pick them she heard a soft tinkle of bells. She stood up and looked about her, wondering if the gnome-boy and his cows were somewhere near. But as there was nothing to be seen, she turned back to the flow-

ers, but she no sooner stretched out her hand to touch them than the bells chimed again. This time she looked more carefully and at last she made out the long solemn faces of three goats watching her from the shadows, one black, one brown and one brindled. Two wore bells around their necks but the brindled one had two little fur tassels instead, hanging under her chin like a pair of silent bells. They had eyes of palest yellow and they stared and stared and stared, until suddenly Lucinda couldn't bear it any longer. Leaving the flowers, she turned and ran out of the wood and down the flowery meadow just as fast as she could go. She felt sure the three goats must be guardians set to watch over the deserted hut and the wood-cutter's enchanted daughter.

She found her parents just packing up to go home for supper. When they got back to the house they found Annali and Gretchen watching for them in a state of great excitement. They seized Lucinda's hands and pulled her around to the barn behind the house, trying to tell her something as they went. They led her into the cow-stall where a single cow was standing. Annali pointed to something lying on the floor and Lucinda stooped down in the dim light and saw that it was a tiny new-born calf.

"Oh the little darling!" she exclaimed, stroking its silky head. "It's the sweetest calf I've ever seen, really the sweetest."

The cow bent her head with a gentle sound just like the cows at home.

"The calf's mother seems to agree with you," laughed Daddy appearing in the doorway.

Annali said they were calling the new calf Ringelblume, which Daddy explained was the German word for marigold. "And Annali says they are going to keep her," he went on. "They usually sell their calves but they find they have just enough pasture to support one more cow and so this calf is to be kept."

"Ringelblume," murmured Lucinda. "What a pretty name. Oh Daddy, may I buy her a bell, a tiny one for a present?"

"If it doesn't cost too much money you may," said Daddy. "But it's time for supper now."

Chapter Four

The next morning there was so much bustle and noise below the balcony that Lucinda could scarcely eat her breakfast. First the boy from the train appeared. He had no cape today and no knapsack.

"Who's that boy?" whispered Lucinda.

"Why, that's Annali's and Gretchen's brother, Johann. Haven't you seen him driving the cows?"

Annali's and Gretchen's brother! So he wasn't a gnome after all! Lucinda was very relieved. Nevertheless, he certainly did carry some extraordinary things on his back. Today it was a basket almost as tall as himself. He slipped it off his shoulders and stood it up under the trees. Then he and Annali and Gretchen began to fill it with all sorts of unexpected things, wooden bowls and spoons and knives, a loaf of bread, and several tins and packages all tumbled in, one on top of another.

29

Then Johann went and fetched a shining scythe and two sickles which he hung in one of the apple trees.

"What can it all be for?" wondered Lucinda.

It was soon explained. There was a knock on their door and Frau Stoppel, the children's mother, came out onto the balcony. She was a big, stout, smiling woman with braided hair and a colorful peasant dress exactly like her daughters'. She now had a long conversation in German with Daddy. But although she pointed several times at Lucinda and then at the enormous basket, and waved her hand toward the hill behind, it was impossible to guess what she was talking about.

"What is she saying?" asked Mommy, when Frau Stoppel paused for breath, for Mommy knew little more German than Lucinda.

"She says that Johann is going to cut the hay in a small pasture up the mountain," answered Daddy. "The children are taking their midday meal and picnicking up there in an empty hut and they would like Lucinda to go with them."

"Oh let me go, please, please say yes!" begged Lucinda.

But Mommy was looking uneasily at the scythe.

"I don't like the looks of that scythe at all," she said. "After all, Johann can't be more than twelve or thirteen himself."

"Oh Mommy!" implored Lucinda.

Daddy turned to Frau Stoppel and explained about the scythe, at which she beamed and waved her hands and spoke again to Daddy.

"She says she doesn't like Ludwig playing with the scythe either," he explained.

"Ludwig!" exclaimed Mommy, "Oh well, if Ludwig is old enough to go, I suppose I can't very well stop Lucinda. But please be sensible, darling."

"I promise I will," said Lucinda as she flew down to join the others. They knew at once by her face that she was to be allowed to go, too, and Gretchen ran for another bowl and spoon which went into the basket with everything else. Johann started to go for another sickle but Daddy shook his head.

At last everyone was ready and Lucinda watched with amazement as Johann hoisted the heavy basket onto his back. Then he unhooked his scythe from the tree and started off. Annali and Gretchen took a sickle each, while Ludwig and Lucinda carried pitchforks.

They followed a narrow zig-zag path that climbed steeply up through the pine woods. Now and then Lucinda caught a glimpse of the Stoppel house and several other chalets, looking like a small toy village in the valley far below. At last they reached the little pasture high among the woods. It was very green and bright with flowers. Lucinda looked at them sadly, wishing they needn't be cut. At the top of the slope stood an empty hut like a miniature chalet.

Johann dropped his basket by the door, then, taking a

whetstone from its wooden case on his belt, he began to sharpen the scythe.

Annali opened the door and the one small window of the hut. Then she and Gretchen began to unpack the basket methodically, arranging everything neatly on any ledge that would serve as a shelf. Lucinda saw by their serious faces that this was no game of "playing house." Today they had become two very responsible people running a proper little home and looking after their family in a really grown-up manner.

The hut had no porch but there was a long wooden step in front, where Annali set out the five bowls in a row and proceeded to divide the food equally into them. There were thin round slices of pink meat and something that looked like purple cabbage, shredded very finely, and a spoonful each of

cold boiled rice and a slice of smooth pale cheese that was full of round holes. Gretchen sliced up the bread with a long sharp knife, while Lucinda buttered it with another. She had never used such a knife before, but after all it was the scythe that Mommy minded, and anyway she was very, very careful. There was milk to drink and a pile of apples and plums from the garden to finish the meal.

When everything was ready they called Johann in from his work and sat in a row on the wooden step to eat. They were all too hungry to do much talking and Lucinda decided that up here it didn't much matter what language you spoke.

When the meal was finished they ran to the edge of the hayfield where they washed their bowls and spoons in a tum-

bling mountain stream, spreading them out on the sunny bank to dry.

Then Johann picked up the scythe and called to his sisters. As Annali turned to go, she said something to Lucinda, pointing her sickle at Ludwig as she spoke. Lucinda guessed that she was being asked to look after him and keep him out of mischief while they worked. So she nodded her head to Annali and held out her hand a little doubtfully to Ludwig. To her surprise he took it and they set off to look for flowers.

They wandered down the hillside and into the woods, picking flowers as they went. Ludwig never stopped talking, but fortunately he did not seem to mind whether she understood or answered his remarks. She was glad of this, for it left her free to dream as she pleased. She imagined herself a beautiful queen turned out of her rightful kingdom with no one to care what became of her except the faithful page at her side. She walked proudly over the moss with her head held high as she fancied a queen would walk, staring into the distance with tragic eyes. But in spite of this she never noticed the woodcutter's hut until they were almost upon it.

Today a whole group of wooden figures stood in a row on the long bench on the porch. They were a little smaller than the girl on the pump but equally lifelike. Lucinda caught her breath. Suppose it was the woodcutter himself who turned people into wood!

And then, too late, she saw the old man sitting in the shadow at the end of the bench. He was smoking the tremendous curly pipe and watching them with small bright eyes. Ludwig saw him too and before she could stop him he slipped his hand from hers and darted onto the porch shouting, "Grossvater! Grossvater!"

Lucinda stood frozen to the spot, expecting to see him turned into wood before her eyes. But to her surprise the old man merely picked him up and sat him on his knee, then turned and smiled at her.

"Guten Morgen," she murmured nervously, not knowing anything else to say.

"Guten Morgen," replied the old man politely, and then most surprisingly he went on in slow, careful English, "You must be the little Miss who is—how do you say it? Holidaying? —in the Stoppel house."

Lucinda nodded her head. She was too astonished to speak.

The old man laughed.

"So! I see you are surprise I speak the English!" he said. "I learn years ago when I was a young men working in Vienna, but I forget much. Perhaps you will come here sometimes and help me speak, please? I am Ludwig's—how do you say 'Grossvater'?—Greatfather? Grandfather?"

"Grossvater," said Ludwig firmly.

"Ludwig's Grandfather!" exclaimed Lucinda. It seemed too good to be true after all her fears. "So you aren't a wood-cutter after all?" she asked, climbing slowly onto the porch.

"Woodcutter? No. I'm a wood carver. See!" and he pointed to the little figures at his side. "But," he went on, "why are you and Ludwig all alone? Where are Annali and Gretchen?"

Lucinda explained that they were cutting hay in the mountain pasture.

"And you," said the old man, leaning toward her eagerly. "Will you come again another day and speak the English with me? Will you do that?"

"Yes I will," she promised. "And please, who is the little lady on your pump?"

"So!" cried Grossvater, pointing his curly pipe at her. "You seen my little Saint Notburga! Was it you, then, who gave her the flowers when I was in Innsbruck yesterday?"

"Yes it was," she answered. "Will you tell me about her please?"

"Next time you come," he replied. "Now off before the others come to find where you are lost."

Lucinda longed to examine the little carved figures on the bench but the old man hustled her out.

"Next time, next time," he said firmly.

When they got back to the pasture they found half the hay already cut and the others getting ready to go. When Lucinda saw them stow everything away in the hut she realized with joy that they must be coming again tomorrow.

When they reached home it was time for supper and bed.
But before going in, Lucinda slipped around to the cow-stall
to say good night to Ringelblume.

Chapter Five

When Lucinda went out to her parents' balcony the next morning, she found them poring over a map.

"What are you doing?" she asked.

"We're planning to go off for a couple of days up one of the mountain valleys," said Mommy. "We hear there's a specially beautiful lake up there." And she pointed it out on the map.

"When are we going?" asked Lucinda apprehensively.

"We hope to be off in a few hours' time," Daddy said.

"Oh but I wanted to go up to the hut again with the others!" cried Lucinda.

"You can go there again when we come back," promised Mommy. "We'll be returning here for a day or so before we start for home."

"But the hay will all be cut by then," cried Lucinda very near tears. "Besides, they need me to look after Ludwig while they're working. And there's Grossvater too, I promised I'd go and talk English with him."

"Grossvater," mused Daddy. "I wonder if that's the old wood carver fellow I met last time I stayed here?"

"That's the one!" exclaimed Lucinda eagerly. "He's Frau Stoppel's father and I promised I'd go and practice English with him. I know! Couldn't I stay here with the Stoppels while you go and paint the lake?"

"That's an idea," said Daddy. "I don't see why you shouldn't, that is, if Frau Stoppel will have you!"

"Oh, but darling . . ." began Mommy looking fussed.

"Oh, come," said Daddy. "I've known the Stoppels for years, they're absolutely reliable. And Lucinda isn't a baby."

"And I promise to do exactly what Frau Stoppel says," put in Lucinda.

"But that's just the trouble," objected Mommy, "You won't understand what she does say!"

Lucinda hadn't thought of that. But she thought of something else.

"There's Lisbet!" she cried triumphantly. "She can't talk any language at all, and Frau Stoppel looks after her all right!"

"That's a point!" laughed Daddy. "And anyway here comes Frau Stoppel herself with the breakfast, so we'll see what she has to say."

The moment Daddy began to speak it was easy to see that Frau Stoppel would be only too pleased to look after Lucinda. She beamed all over her friendly face and nodded her head until her silver earrings jingled. When Daddy had translated her many assurances even Mommy stopped looking anxious and Lucinda hugged her with delight.

"Sure you won't mind having no one to talk to?" asked Daddy teasingly. "I seem to remember you're rather a chatter-box sometimes!"

But Lucinda had already learned several German words, and she found she could almost always understand Annali and Gretchen and sometimes even forgot they spoke a different language. So she only laughed and said, "Quite sure. Besides, you've forgotten Grossvater. I can go and speak English to him!"

"So you can!" laughed Daddy. "Well you'll be all right then. And now here's some money to buy that bell for Ringelblume." He handed her two shining 5 schilling pieces.

"Each of these is worth about twenty cents," he told her, "but that should be enough for a bell and you can keep the change if there is any."

Johann had one or two jobs to do in the cow-stall after breakfast and Ludwig was sent down the road with a message.

"It doesn't look as though we'll be starting to the hayfield very early today," observed Lucinda who was keeping a look-out from the balcony. "Do you think there'd be time to buy the bell before we go? Oh, Daddy, would you come down with me and ask the others?" she begged. "And then if there is time p'raps one of them might show me the way to the shop."

Daddy was in the middle of sorting paints and canvasses, but he got up obligingly and followed her downstairs and out into the garden.

"How are you going to manage when I'm not here to ask

your questions for you?" he teased, but Lucinda only laughed.

They found the two little girls preparing Lisbet's bath. But when Daddy explained what Lucinda wanted Annali nodded to Gretchen who put down the bucket she was carrying, and, wiping her hands on her apron, stood ready to start at once.

"You're in luck," remarked Daddy. "They say there's plenty of time and Gretchen will take you to the cowbell shop right away. Got your money?"

For answer Lucinda opened her hand where the two large coins lay shining, then she hurried out of the gate after Gretchen.

They ran down the road and over the swaying bridge and into the village street. The shop was on a corner near the bridge, and they paused for a moment to look in the window

which was full of exciting things, flower brooches and wooden toys and caps and belts embroidered with alpine flowers. Right across the front of the window a row of gold-painted bells were arranged according to size. The smallest ones were marked six schillings each.

When they got inside the shop they found they were not the only customers; two tall gray-haired Englishwomen were there before them, examining a dozen dolls in Tirolean costume, spread out on the counter for them to see. To Lucinda's surprise they did not seem quite satisfied, and while the shopkeeper rummaged in an inner room the elder lady murmured, "You know these are just the same as those we saw in Innsbruck. Now that is what I really want," she added, catching sight of Gretchen who was wandering about the shop. "I want a doll dressed exactly like that little girl in the everyday costume of the district. Just look at that delightful embroidered bodice—I'd gladly give three or four hundred schillings for a doll dressed just like that."

"Perhaps you'll find one in Salzburg next week," suggested her companion.

"Maybe I will. Anyway, in the meantime I'll buy a couple of these because they are very charming, although not what I'm really looking for."

Lucinda edged a little closer and was pleased when the lady chose her own especial favorites, one with a headdress like a golden halo fixed to her gold-lace cap, and another with a tiny gold-lace topknot like a funny little crown perched on her braided hair. Both dolls wore full black skirts and aprons

44

of flowered silk Lucinda privately thought their clothes far more exciting than Gretchen's and wondered what lucky little girls were going to receive such gorgeous presents.

"I expect they must be for her grandchildren, because she looks rather old," she decided, gazing up at the gray-haired woman who now handed the dolls to the shopkeeper.

"Will you send them to me please at my hotel?" she asked. "Miss Carmichael, Hotel Edelweiss."

Now it was the children's turn to be served, and as soon as the dolls were put away in their boxes the shopkeeper brought out all the small-sized bells in the shop and waited patiently while Gretchen and Lucinda rang every one in turn to see which had the sweetest tone. They made their choice at last

and Lucinda handed over her two 5-schilling pieces. She had four schillings change, and it looked like a lot of money.

As they went up the road toward the house, Mommy and

Daddy came out of the gate with their knapsacks and painting things.

"Ah, I hoped we'd meet you!" cried Mommy. "Now listen, darling. Although the Stoppels don't speak English, nearly all the shopkeepers in the village do, so remember, any one of them will help you if you're in any kind of difficulty with the language."

"And there's Grossvater, too," Lucinda reminded her, "He just loves talking English and I'm going to see him today."

"So you're really sure you'll be all right?" asked Mommy, still a trifle anxious.

"Positive," replied Lucinda.

"Of course she'll be all right," said Daddy. "What I want to know is, did you get that bell?"

"Here it is!" cried Lucinda pulling it out of its bag. "It had the sweetest tone of them all—listen!" and she rang it for them to hear. She rang them down the road as far as the bridge, where the soft bell notes were drowned in the roar of the tumbling river.

Ringelblume wasn't quite old enough to start wearing her bell just yet, but Lucinda took it around to the cowstall and rang it for her to hear.

"I'll come and ring it to you every evening at bedtime," she promised, "so you'll get used to the sound."

Chapter Six

Johann was ready at last and the children set off up the zig-zag path through the woods. As it was already late they unpacked their lunch as soon as they arrived and sat down on the step of the little hut to eat it right away. As soon as the meal was over and the dishes washed and set out in the sun to dry, Ludwig looked up questioningly at Lucinda.

"Grossvater?" he asked.

She nodded and took him by the hand and they set off together for the little hut in the wood.

The old man was sitting outside on the porch, carving a little dancing peasant girl with a wide-brimmed hat and swirling skirts.

"So!" he cried delightedly. "You come again to see me and speak English. That is very good!"

Ludwig walked straight indoors, but Lucinda stopped to look at the little figures on the bench, a shepherd boy, and an angel, and the unfinished dancer.

"We better go first and settle Ludwig," Grossvater remarked and led the way into the hut.

They found Ludwig standing stolidly in the middle of the dark little room staring up at a narrow shelf high above his head. And no wonder he was staring, for the shelf held a wonderful procession of men and animals all carefully carved and painted.

"Did you make them?" Lucinda asked.

"Oh no," Grossvater said, smiling. "They are many years older than I am. My father's grossvater made them when my father himself was a little boy like Ludwig. It shows the return from the alpine pastures. See, here is the *hausfrau* outside her house, churning butter to feed the hungry ones on their return. And this is the pump of her house. Here are the goats and sheep and cows who have been in the high pastures during the summer months, and here are the men with the horses and carts at the end.

He lifted them down one by one as he spoke and set them out in order along a bench built against the wall. When they were all in position Ludwig went and stood in front of them, pointing to each in turn and murmuring to himself in a sing-song voice.

"He'll be happy now," said the old man. "Now you come outside and see my little Saint Notburga." He pronounced the name so softly that it sound like "Nopura."

He led the way around to the back of the hut where the sunlight fell full on the wooden pump, brightening the faded colors of the little figure and putting a sparkle into the falling water.

"How gentle she looks," said Lucinda looking up at the little saint's face. "Please tell me all about her."

"This is her story," said Grossvater coming to lean against the wooden pedestal on which the figure stood. "She was a simple kitchen maid and she lived in these parts hundreds of years ago. She was very good and kindhearted and always she saved what was left from her master's table and from her own meals to feed the poor."

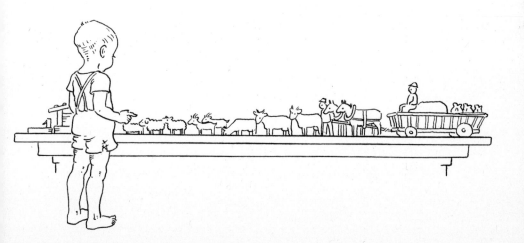

"So that's why she has such a gentle face," murmured Lucinda, dabbling her fingers in the water.

"But her master was not kind-hearted," Grossvater continued, "and he ordered her to give no more food to the poor. This was more than the little maid could bear, so she left and went to another post. But once again she found herself working for a hard master. This time it was one who made her work overtime and would not allow her to go to church and worship God as she wished to do. There came a certain Sunday evening when the church bell rang the Angelus while she was still kept at work in the fields.

" 'God shall decide!' she cried suddenly, and she tossed her sickle into the air. And there it remained for a long while, suspended in the air as though it were hanging on an invisible hook."

"What a wonderful thing to happen," breathed Lucinda, staring at him wide-eyed.

"It was a miracle straight from God," replied Grossvater, "and because of it you will see many figures of Saint Notburga in shrines and churches in this part of Tirol, and paintings too, on the walls of many houses. You will know her, for always she has her sickle, and sometimes also a sheaf of wheat or a loaf of bread to feed the poor."

"I did see her!" interrupted Lucinda eagerly. "It must have been her, throwing her sickle into the air like you said. I saw her from the train on a house down the valley the day we came to Tirol."

"That's right," said the old man nodding slowly. "You will

50

see her, too, on other pumps like mine. That's why I carved her for my own pump here in the woods."

For a minute or two Lucinda stood trailing her fingers in the water and watching the rippled reflection of the little saint as she thought over the story she had heard. Then she turned to the old man with another question. "Do you live here all by yourself in this little hut?"

"All by myself with my three goats. Perhaps you see them in the woods?"

Lucinda nodded but did not speak, feeling ashamed when she remembered how much the goats had frightened her.

"But in winter," Grossvater continued, "when the snow comes and it is very kalt—how do you say it? Cold?—then I go down to my daughter's house, the Stoppel house where you stay, and there I spend the winter months. But this place is best for my work of carving wood."

"What do you do with the carvings?" asked Lucinda.

"I take them to a shop in Innsbruck where they sell them to foreign visitors. But they do not want very many, and some they cannot sell. The people have not the money and so they buy instead the cheap things that anybody can make."

"Saint Notburga's the one I'd want to buy," Lucinda remarked, smiling up at the little figure, "but then of course she's not for sale."

"Ah, hark!" exclaimed Grossvater suddenly. "Do you hear them coming, my three beautiful goats?"

As the three goats trotted toward them, Lucinda fancied she saw a look of amusement in their pale yellow eyes. How glad she was that they couldn't tell Grossvater how foolishly she had run away on the day she first met them.

"Why hasn't this one got a bell?" she asked as the brindled one came near.

"She needs no bell, she has two of her own," laughed Grossvater pointing to the brindled tassels.

"Have they got names?" she asked him next.

"Indeed yes, their names are Barbeli, Zozel, and Isa. The brindled one is Zozel."

And then he laughed as Zozel broke away from Lucinda and made her way around to the porch, followed by the other two. "There they go!" he chuckled. "They know the time without any clocks. Each day I give them something to eat at this time, and the bucket is kept on the porch—they know!"

As soon as the goats had finished their meal they trotted away through the trees and the sound of their bells grew fainter and fainter until they tinkled into silence. Lucinda and Grossvater sat on the porch and she told him about her parents and her home. As they talked, he worked steadily at the little dancing girl, deftly notching the frilled edge of her petticoat with his knife.

"Hark!" he said suddenly lifting his head. "Hear it?"

Lucinda listened and heard a strange call rising and falling in the still mountain air.

"Whatever is it?" she asked.

"That is Johann—he must be calling for you and Ludwig."

"Johann—calling in that funny high sort of voice?" questioned Lucinda in surprise.

It was Grossvater's turn to look puzzled.

"Did you never hear anyone yodel before?" he asked incredulously. "So! I will answer him." To Lucinda's amazement he raised his voice and sent the same strange high-pitched call echoing through the trees in reply. "Yodeling, that is the sound to carry up here in the mountains," he explained. "So now

you will have to go. I had not noticed it was so late. Look at the shadows up there on the hillside. But first here is something to take back for the haymakers' tea, and one each for yourself and Ludwig." As he spoke he reached up and picked five yellow pears from a tree which grew against the porch.

They found Ludwig still brooding over the wooden animals, but as soon as he saw the pears his interest switched to them and he held out a small fat hand.

"Please come back another day and speak with me again," said Grossvater as he saw them off.

When they reached the hayfield they found the others putting away their tools and getting ready to leave. Lucinda saw with satisfaction that one small corner of hay still remained to be cut.

"So we'll be coming again tomorrow I expect," she thought happily.

Grossvater was right. It was getting late and twilight began to close about them as they dipped down into the woods, and by the time the path zig-zagged into the open again the first lights twinkled below in the valley.

Chapter Seven

There were no errands or odd jobs to be done next morning so the haymaking party got off to an early start. As soon as they reached the hill pasture, the three elder children set to work on the section of hay still standing.

Ludwig had collected a handful of small pebbles on his way up through the woods, and he now spread these out in a corner of the hut and was soon absorbed in some secret game of his own.

Lucinda, wondering what to do with herself, suddenly decided that she would get lunch ready as a surprise for the haymakers when they came in from their work. So she collected the wooden bowls from the shelf inside the hut, then she unpacked the basket of food Frau Stoppel had provided. Getting out the long sharp knife, she set to work, cutting and spreading and dividing the food as she had seen the others do.

55

When all was ready, she carried the five plates out to the step.
As she was putting the last one down she heard a shout of
triumph from the lower end of the hayfield, and looked up
just in time to see the final green swath fall before Johann's
scythe. There were exclamations of delight when the others
got back and found the meal all ready, and although Lucinda
could not understand a word they said, she knew they were
very pleased.

Ludwig ate with one hand only and with the other he continued to play with his pebbles, murmuring to himself between mouthfuls. But as soon as the meal was over he seemed
to remember Lucinda, and turning to her eagerly he asked
his usual question, "Grossvater?"

But to Lucinda's surprise Johann shook his head decidedly,
and she realized that he had some plan for the afternoon in
which she was to be included. So she watched with great interest as he made his way around to the side of the hut and
unhitched some odd-looking crosses from the wall. Each was
made with a tall central stake and two or three crossbars
fastened at different heights and angles. He carried these out

56

to the hayfield and hammered them upright into the ground until they stood securely. Then he returned for another load and Lucinda saw that there was a large number of crosses ranged against the wall of the hut under the shelter of the roof. Now Annali and Gretchen joined her and they all three helped to carry the crosses out to the field, where Johann stood them in rows. When all the crosses were in place Gretchen ran into the hut and returned with four long pitchforks which she handed around.

When Ludwig saw there was no fork for him, he dropped his pebbles and, opening his mouth, let out one long howl. Johann scolded him angrily, trying to persuade him to go back to his scattered pebbles. But Annali disappeared behind the hut where they heard her rummaging about and presently she returned triumphantly with the stump of a broken pitchfork, which she gave to the wailing Ludwig, turning his tears to immediate smiles.

Johann now explained to Lucinda with many expressive gestures how the wet, cut hay in the field must all be dried, and he showed her how to fork it onto the crosses, spreading it out on the bars so that the wind might blow through and dry it. Then he showed her how to pile it up and up until there was nothing to be seen but a queer high-piled haystack, standing on a single leg.

She soon grasped the knack of it and found herself keeping pace with the others, while Ludwig manfully did his share, piling hay with his broken fork onto the lower cross-bars, which were all that he could reach.

They worked steadily all the afternoon, but the sun was already low in the sky before the last cross was covered and the final handful of hay scraped up from the stubble.

As they started for home in the evening light, Lucinda looked back over her shoulder and thought the queer tall

stacks with their long shadows looked like a crowd of mysterious people, and she fancied that as soon as she was out of sight they would all troop slowly across the field and take possession of the little hut.

As they followed the downward path through the woods Johann began to sing a lilting song with a yodeling chorus in which his sisters joined. By the second verse Lucinda had caught the rhythmic tune and was able to sing with the others, although she had no words and could not attempt the soaring yodel at the end. By the third verse Ludwig also decided to sing. But he chose to sing quite different words to a tuneless chant of his own.

But when they got home to the Stoppel house all the joy went out of the day.

They found Frau Stoppel in the kitchen surrounded by the childrens' old boots and winter clothes. She looked up unhappily as they all trooped in and said something that Lucinda could not understand. For a moment the children stood in horrified silence, then they all burst out talking together. The only word Lucinda could understand was "Ringelblume" which they all said over and over again. Frau Stoppel looked quite distracted, waving her hands toward the shoes on the floor. Ludwig and Gretchen began to cry, while Annali flopped down on the floor and tried desperately to squeeze her bare feet into boots that were far too small.

"What is it? Oh what has happened?" cried Lucinda frantically, discovering suddenly that she didn't know so very much German after all. It was all very well for playing games

59

but no good when it came to something that really mattered like this. What could all these clothes have to do with Ringelblume? Now Annali was crying, too, so it must be something terrible. Perhaps Ringelblume was ill or even dead!

She slipped out of the kitchen and hurried around to the cow-stall where the little calf greeted her as usual, eagerly trying to suck her outstretched fingers. It was easy to see she was perfectly well. Lucinda felt more bewildered than ever.

"I know! Grossvater, he'll explain," she thought suddenly, and running back to the kitchen she seized the astonished Gretchen by the hand and urged her to come outside.

"Please come with me to Grossvater," she begged, "and

tell him what's happening to Ringelblume so that he can explain to me."

61

Gretchen, far too miserable to understand or to care where she went, allowed Lucinda to drag her up through the woods.

Grossvater was just finishing his supper out on the porch and was very surprised when Lucinda panted up the steps pulling the tearful Gretchen after her. She explained why they had come and Grossvater drew Gretchen gently toward him and asked her what had happened. Between her sobs she poured out a long story. When she had finished Grossvater turned to Lucinda.

"Well, it seems," he said slowly, "that although they have pasture to keep the calf, the children have grown too much, and there is not enough money to buy all the new boots and winter clothes they will need."

"So that's why Annali tried to squeeze into her last year's boots," interrupted Lucinda.

"Undoubtedly," agreed Grossvater. "Anyway, their mother has decided that it will be necessary after all to sell the calf for money to buy new clothes."

"Oh no!" cried Lucinda in horror. "Not sell Ringelblume when we love her so much! Besides, we've even got her bell and she knows the sound of it already."

"I know," said the old man with a sigh. "It is sad because the children had been told this calf was to keep, and so they had come to love it. It is hard, but that is the trouble with being poor. I know, because I am poor, too. But the pasture will remain, and if this calf pays for the winter boots no doubt they will keep the next one instead."

Lucinda felt too miserable to reply. What was the use of the next calf, when it was Ringelblume they loved? She remembered that she had 4 schillings left over from Ringelblume's bell.

"How many schillings does it take to buy winter boots?" she asked.

"Hundreds," said Grossvater briefly.

She remembered something else. "That English lady!" she burst out. "She said she'd give three hundred schillings for a doll dressed just like Gretchen. Oh, Gretchen, have you got a doll we could dress?"

It was Gretchen's turn to look bewildered, and Grossvater, too, was puzzled. When Lucinda explained about the two Englishwomen in the shop he shook his head.

"Gretchen would certainly have no doll that would sell for three hundred schillings," he said decidedly, "and how would you dress it anyhow?"

Lucinda hadn't thought of that part of the problem.

"But," the old man continued thoughtfully, "I think this has given me the beginning of an idea. No! No! I'll not tell you yet. You go home now. I can't think it out with you two around asking questions. You go back and have your suppers now and come back in the morning as soon as you've had breakfast. Understand? Now off you go, and don't you worry too much about that calf."

Grossvater hadn't promised anything, he hadn't even told them his plan, and yet they went home through the dusky

63

wood with very hopeful hearts. However, they did not quite dare take the little bell out to the stall that night in case Ringelblume might never wear it after all.

Chapter Eight

Nobody went to the hayfield next morning so Lucinda and Gretchen were free to run up to Grossvater right after breakfast. They found him out on the porch, fixing movable arms and legs to a beautifully carved wooden doll. They stood and watched in silence while he finished the job. When it was done he looked up with a smile.

"For your English lady," he explained, handing the doll to Lucinda.

"Oh, Grossvater!" she gasped, turning it around to study every detail, from the perfect little hands and feet to the delicately carved head with its coronet of braids.

"How did you ever carve her hair?" she questioned. "It's just like Gretchen's—and her face, oh how I love her face! I like her even better than the dancing girl or any of the others."

"Better than Saint Notburga?" asked Grossvater with a twinkle in his eye.

"Ah, no!" cried Lucinda quickly. "But then, nobody could ever be as nice as Saint Notburga! But how did you make this one so quickly? Did you stay up all night?"

The old man nodded, smiling.

"And who minds a night now and then," he said, "when there's something important to do? But now you must listen to the rest of the plan. First I will tell it to you in English, and then I will tell it to Gretchen in German. It is this. I have a sister Anna who is a very clever needlewoman, no one in all Tirol could dress the doll better than Anna. But there is not much time if the English lady is going to Salzburg next week, and Anna is a busy woman; she has little tables out in her garden where she serves kaffe—coffee do you call it in English? Now you and Gretchen would have to do Tante Anna's work and serve her customers, while she makes clothes for the doll. Would you be able to do that?"

"You mean carry out the cups on little trays like real waitresses? Oh, what fun!" cried Lucinda, hopping with excitement. She could scarcely stand still while he explained the plan to Gretchen, and as soon as he stopped for breath she broke in excitedly, "How do we get there? When can we start?" while Gretchen asked eager questions in German.

"Wait! Wait!" cried Grossvater, clapping his hands to his ears. "I will tell you all if only you will let me speak. First of all you will need two schillings each for the Autobus—have you got two schillings?"

"I've got four left over from Ringelblume's bell," said Lucinda. "Two for each of us, isn't that lucky? Can we start at once?"

"You get the Autobus by the bridge at 12 o'clock," said Grossvater. "Gretchen knows. Now you'd better be off, you'll want something to eat before you go."

He wrapped the doll in a newspaper and thrust it into Lucinda's arms, scarcely waiting for their thanks as he hurried them on their way.

They ran all the way home and burst into the kitchen full of excitement. Lucinda unwrapped the doll while Gretchen explained Grossvater's plan to Annali and her mother. But Frau Stoppel merely shrugged her shoulders when she saw the doll. It was easy to see that she couldn't believe anyone would really give all that good money for a doll. However she agreed to let Gretchen go with Lucinda provided Annali stayed home to help with the little ones.

The two set off after an early lunch. There were so many people waiting for the bus that Lucinda wondered how they would all get in. And indeed when the crowd began to move, she and Gretchen were pushed to the back so that there were no seats left when they got to the door of the bus. But the driver unexpectedly produced two smooth round logs of wood from behind his seat and these he stood on end in the aisle like two tree stumps, signing to the children to sit on them.

"We might as well be sitting in a forest," thought Lucinda with amusement, as she settled down.

It was an exciting drive and rather terrifying too, for the

67

road wound up a narrow gorge with a mountain rising up to the sky on one side of the road and on the other a swirling river so far below that Lucinda preferred not to look. She wondered what would happen if they met another bus, but luckily none came.

Presently they rattled over a rickety bridge and the gorge widened into a valley with a few brown chalets dotted about in low green fields by the river. Here Gretchen asked the driver to stop and she and Lucinda got out. They walked along a riverside path until they came to a tiny chalet with three little tables out in front, covered with green and white cloths.

Lucinda had never seen so many flowers all crowded together. They hung in garlands from the balcony and climbed around the windows and door, while the gaint sunflowers in the garden grew as high as the roof. And as though there were not enough color already, there were blue glass balls like Christmas tree decorations stuck on sticks in the flower beds.

Lucinda was reminded of the story of the Snow Queen.

"It might be the old woman's cottage in the enchanted garden," she thought. "That was by a river too."

And then Tante Anna opened the door and Lucinda's heart skipped a beat. She was dressed in black from head to foot except for a tarnished gold tassel in front of her high-crowned hat. Lucinda remembered Hansel and Gretel and the gingerbread house. A little cold shiver trickled down her back.

And then quite unexpectedly the little old woman smiled and took off her high-crowned hat, and Lucinda wondered why the thought of a witch had ever crossed her mind. She's much more like a Fairy Godmother really, she thought comfortably, as she followed Gretchen onto the porch.

Tante Anna was delighted to see them and had so many questions to ask that it was some time before Gretchen could explain about Ringelblume. But when she did the little old lady seemed very kind and understanding. She took the doll out of its wrappings and studied it thoughtfully for a minute or two as though deciding what it should wear. Then all in a moment she seemed to make up her mind. She bustled indoors and came out with a workbox full of scraps of lace and odds and ends of material. There was red cloth for a bodice and black for a skirt and even a small piece of the blue and white patterned material of which Gretchen's apron had been made. Lucinda began to wonder if perhaps Tante Anna herself made the clothes that Annali and Gretchen wore. As she watched, Tante Anna took a pair of scissors out of her workbox and set to work, ex-

plaining meanwhile to Gretchen what she and Lucinda must do to help, while she herself was busy with the doll.

First of all the kitchen table and bench must be scrubbed, and the freshly laundered sheets and towels dampened to help them bleach. Gretchen ran to the kitchen and got to work with the scrubbing brush while Lucinda took out the big watering can and sprinkled the sheets which were spread out on the sunny grass.

Suddenly the gate clicked and she looked up to see two men come in with bulging knapsacks and heavy climbing boots. They slung their knapsacks onto the grass and sat down at the nearest table.

Tante Anna never paused in her sewing but shouted to Gretchen, who came out at once and took the order. She looked wonderfully businesslike and Lucinda was very much impressed.

Gretchen's next job was to take some boxes of apples and pears to be sold in the village shop. Lucinda watched her enviously, wishing that she might go as well and push the funny wheelbarrow, but of course she had to stay in case any more customers came.

And no sooner had Gretchen disappeared than somebody else did come, another young man with a knapsack. Lucinda hung back uncertainly, but Tante Anna nodded encouragement from the porch. So she went bravely up to the young man and managed to say, "Bitte?" She knew that this meant, "Please?" She wondered anxiously how she was going to understand his answer, but to her relief he simply asked for

"Milch in Glas"—a glass of milk, one of the things she really did understand because she had it for supper every night in the Stoppel house. She raced to the kitchen, took a glass from the cupboard and filled it from a jug that Gretchen had left on the table. She stood the glass on a small metal tray and carried it out, while Tante Anna nodded approvingly from the porch. She felt just like a real, professional waitress!

However, she was thankful to see Gretchen returning ahead of the next group of customers, a family party this time, and it was easy to guess that they would want a good deal more than "Milch in Glas." They certainly did want more and the two little girls were kept busy running to and fro fetching all the food and drink they ordered.

When everyone was settled, Tante Anna sent Gretchen indoors on one last errand while Lucinda hurried across to the porch to see how the doll was getting on. She was already dressed in her underclothes and Tante Anna was busily stitching lace around the short puffed sleeves of her little blouse.

Presently Gretchen appeared on the porch carrying a wonderful chocolate cake on a tray, together with a jug of steam-

ing coffee and three cups and saucers. She put the tray on the table at Tante Anna's elbow and sat down on the bench beside Lucinda.

For a while Lucinda's whole attention was concentrated on her cake. She had never eaten anything quite so good before. It was the kind of cake that melted in your mouth, and was served with a great frothy mound of rich whipped cream heaped on the plate beside it. Only when she had scraped up the final crumbs and licked the last scrap of cream from her fork did she turn her attention to the other two. They were talking so earnestly that she found herself wishing she could understand their language. Tante Anna spoke emphatically, pointing to the doll, but the only word Lucinda could distinguish was "Morgen" while Gretchen sat with her fork in the air and a worried look in her eyes as she said something about the Autobus.

Lucinda looked from one to the other, trying to puzzle it out. She knew that although "Guten Morgen" was "good morning" the word "Morgen" all by itself meant "tomorrow." So, as the doll's clothes were not finished yet, she could only suppose that Tante Anna was suggesting they should come again tomorrow which seemed the nicest possible idea. So why should Gretchen look worried, and what was the trouble about the Autobus?

Why of course! Lucinda suddenly understood. They had used up all their money today and had no schillings left for the Autobus tomorrow.

But there was no further chance to discuss it now, for the

customers began calling for their bills. Lucinda watched admiringly as Gretchen went calmly from table to table, collecting the customers' schillings and working out their change. As she counted the money into Tante Anna's hand Lucinda went out across the grass and began to clear the deserted tables. She was lifting the last plate from the family's table when something clinked against the china and there on the cloth lay four bright schillings. Once again she felt like a real waitress as she gathered up the unexpected tip and ran with it to Tante Anna. But to her surprise the old lady shook her head and waved the coins away, clearly explaining without any words that they were intended for Gretchen and Lucinda.

Gretchen gave a shrill little squeal of delight, and seizing Lucinda's two hands whirled her away in a wild dance, shouting excitedly all the while, "Autobus—Autobus—Autobus!" until it suddenly dawned on Lucinda that here was an end of their worries—four bright schillings to pay for their Autobus tickets tomorrow!

Chapter Nine

Tante Anna was already at work on the porch when Gretchen and Lucinda arrived at her chalet the next day. When Lucinda saw the doll she wondered if Tante Anna had also been up all night to do so much exquisite work. Everything was finished except the little red bodice on which Tante Anna was working now, embroidering the many-colored design in tiny, tiny stitches.

Today there was fruit to be picked and carried indoors in addition to serving the customers, and Lucinda and Gretchen had a busy afternoon. The time flew by so quickly that Lucinda could scarcely believe it when Tante Anna called from the porch, and she ran to find coffee and cakes already laid out on the table.

The doll was finished; she might have been Gretchen's twin. She even had tiny silver earrings and a silver bead like a locket on a thin black cord around her neck.

"So!" remarked Tante Anna, as she wrapped the doll in tissue paper and put her into a box. Lucinda longed to be able to speak Tante Anna's language so that she could thank her properly. But from the twinkly way the old lady smiled it seemed that she understood without any words, so perhaps she really was a Fairy Godmother after all!

It was nearly dark when the bus got back to the village and they were glad to find Annali waiting on the bridge to meet them. They showed her the doll by the light from the bell shop window, and then they set off for the Hotel Edelweiss.

It was an imposing place and they went up the steps a little timidly. Gretchen and Lucinda waited in the doorway, while Annali went bravely toward the reception desk and asked for Miss Carmichael. The girl at the desk glanced hastily at the clock, and a lot of talk followed in which the only word that Lucinda could catch was "Bahnhof" and that she knew meant station. Now Annali also turned to the clock with an anxious look on her face, and Lucinda guessed that something had gone wrong with their plan.

In a minute Annali came running toward them gabbling something about Miss Carmichael and Salzburg and Bahnhof, then she and Gretchen seized Lucinda's hands and swept her out of the hotel and down the steps and into the village street where they ran and ran and ran. Lucinda tried to puzzle it out as she panted along between them, and she could only suppose that Miss Carmichael had decided to go on to Salzburg this week instead of next.

"We've just got to catch her before she leaves!" she thought wildly, trying to run faster than ever.

When they turned into the road that led to the station they had to let go of one another's hands and dodge through the crowd pouring out of a train that had just arrived.

"Hullo! Hullo! What's the hurry?" cried a familiar voice, and the next moment Lucinda was swept off her feet and into her father's arms.

"Daddy! Mommy!" she cried delightedly, and then, "But I've got to hurry. We must catch Miss Carmichael at the Bahnhof before the train goes out—at least I think that's why we're running, anyway it's terribly important."

"It sounds most mysterious," laughed Daddy, releasing her.

The little train was in the station and it did not take them long to spot Miss Carmichael standing at one of the lighted carriage windows.

This time it was Lucinda who did the talking. She took the doll out of its wrappings and made her way toward Miss Carmichael, wondering how to begin. But it was Miss Carmichael herself who opened the conversation. She no sooner caught sight of the doll in Lucinda's arms than she leaned out of the window and exclaimed, "Oh where in the world did you get that beautiful doll?"

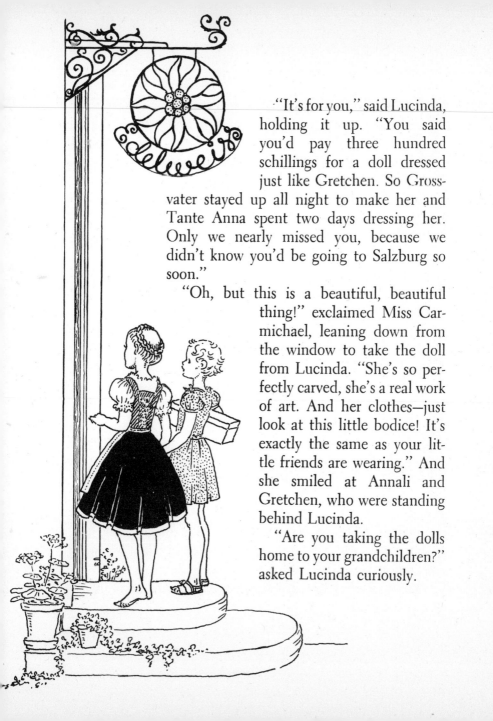

"It's for you," said Lucinda, holding it up. "You said you'd pay three hundred schillings for a doll dressed just like Gretchen. So Grossvater stayed up all night to make her and Tante Anna spent two days dressing her. Only we nearly missed you, because we didn't know you'd be going to Salzburg so soon."

"Oh, but this is a beautiful, beautiful thing!" exclaimed Miss Carmichael, leaning down from the window to take the doll from Lucinda. "She's so perfectly carved, she's a real work of art. And her clothes—just look at this little bodice! It's exactly the same as your little friends are wearing." And she smiled at Annali and Gretchen, who were standing behind Lucinda.

"Are you taking the dolls home to your grandchildren?" asked Lucinda curiously.

"No indeed!" laughed Miss Carmichael, "I haven't any grandchildren. And anyhow these dolls aren't for children at all. They are for my own collection. I have hundreds of dolls, collected from all over the world, and when I'm at home in England I take them around in a large van and show them in schools and village halls, while I lecture about the countries from which they come. But tell me something," she went on. "How is it that you are selling this doll? You aren't an Austrian child."

"Oh no," said Lucinda, "But I'm staying here with Annali and Gretchen and we need the money for Ringelblume." And she told the story of the little calf.

"What a perfectly charming story!" said Miss Carmichael. "Now every time I show this doll I shall tell the story of Ringelblume."

And partly because of Ringelblume and partly because the doll was lovelier than any she had seen before, she gave them five hundred schillings, instead of three.

They were so overwhelmed at the sight of so much money that for a moment they even forgot their thanks, then they all looked up together with beaming faces.

"Oh, THANK YOU!" cried Lucinda, while the others echoed:

"Danke! Danke! Danke schön!"

They were all startled by a sudden shrill whistle from the little engine.

"Whee-oooo-ee-oo!" it whooped, and immediately the train began to move.

78

Miss Carmichael leaned out of the window to wave to them and they ran along the platform until the little toy train outdistanced them, and with one last whistle, like a gay triumphant laugh, it chugged off into the dark.

Annali took charge of the money as she was the eldest of the three, and they turned away from the station hand in hand.

As they made their way up the village street, Lucinda was reminded of the night of her arrival. The flower-filled windows were lighted again and a snatch of song came echoing through the darkness. But there was one tremendous difference, for then she had come as a stranger, but now she felt so much a part of it all that she never even noticed the roar of the river as they ran over the swaying bridge.

They burst into the Stoppel kitchen, breathlessly triumphant, and Annali thrust the five hundred schillings into her mother's lap. Frau Stoppel stared unbelievingly, counting and re-counting it until at last she looked up with a smile that sent Annali and Gretchen dancing about the kitchen, yodeling with joy.

"Daddy!" called Lucinda running to the door. "Please could you come down here for a minute? I'm almost sure from their faces that Ringelblume is safe, but please will you ask Frau Stoppel to make quite, quite sure?"

"All is well!" announced Daddy, after a word with the children's smiling mother. "Frau Stoppel says that now she has all this money toward the winter clothes, they will most certainly keep the calf!"

79

"Hooray!" shouted Lucinda happily, whirling about the kitchen with the others. But suddenly she pulled up short.

"I must go and tell Grossvater, he'll be so pleased," she exclaimed, making for the door.

"Oh, darling, not tonight!" called Mommy from the stairs.

"But Mommy, it's all Grossvater's doing," explained Lucinda. "You see, if he hadn't thought of the plan and worked all night Ringelblume would have been sold."

"I'm truly sorry darling, but I can't let you go tonight," replied Mommy, appearing in the doorway. "Just look at the time. It's nearly eight and you're going to be all tomorrow night in the train and most of the following day as well."

"But Mommy . . ." began Lucinda pleadingly.

"I tell you what!" said Daddy, coming to the rescue as he so often did. "I'll go and call on Grossvater tonight. I want to see him anyway. I'll explain that you wanted to come yourself but I know he'll understand when he hears about tomorrow's journey. Of course I won't say why you wanted to come, I'll leave you to tell him the news yourself in the morning. How will that be?"

"Oh, Daddy, that will be perfect," said Lucinda. And before she knew it, she was yawning, and suddenly aware that Mommy was right and bed would be good after all.

Chapter Ten

As Lucinda climbed up through the sun-dappled wood the next morning she heard a sound of chopping, and when she reached the hut she found Grossvater busy splitting up logs and stacking them neatly against the wall of the hut.

"Guten Morgen!" she shouted, as soon as she was near enough to make herself heard.

"Guten Morgen indeed!" reproved the old man, as he straightened up and looked at her with a twinkle. "And what is wrong with 'Good-morning,' don't we always speak English together, you and I?"

81

"Oh, I'm sorry Grossvater!" laughed Lucinda. "But actually, it's lucky we do speak English because I've got some very exciting news which I *can* only tell you in English anyway."

"And what is this exciting news?" he enquired.

"It's about the doll—Miss Carmichael was so thrilled with her that she gave us five hundred schillings and Ringelblume is saved."

"Five hundred schillings," mused the old man. "That is a lot of money."

"It's because the doll was so 'specially lovely. She called it a work of art."

"She really said that?" cried Grossvater, very much pleased. "Ach, then I am glad indeed that she has the doll."

"She nearly didn't get it," Lucinda said, remembering, and she told him how they had only just managed to catch Miss Carmichael at the station.

"And Anna, did she make the clothes?" he asked.

"Oh yes, and they were simply perfect with tiny silver earrings and the bodice all covered with embroidery and lace on the sleeves and everything. And Gretchen and I had a wonderful time being waitresses and looking after the customers." She settled down on a pile of logs and told him the whole story from start to finish.

The old man listened attentively, nodding from time to time and only interrupting when she became excited and talked so fast that he couldn't follow.

"But now I will have to say good-by," she said sadly, when all their adventures had been told. "You see, we are starting home on this evening's train. Oh, I wish we didn't have to go!"

"Well, this won't be quite good-by," he said, "because I shall come down to the station to see you off this evening."

"Oh, Grossvater, will you? How lovely!" she cried, feeling cheered at once. "But I must go and say good-by to Saint Notburga anyway." And she got up and went around to the back of the hut. She stood for a long while looking up at the little saint, noting every detail until she knew she would always remember the way she looked standing there in the sunlight with the mountains rising behind her into a cloudless sky.

When Lucinda left the hut, Grossvater stood on the porch and waved every time she looked back until at last the trees hid him from view. Then he returned to his work and the companionable sound of his chop-chop-chopping followed her down through the trees.

When she came to the edge of the wood she saw her father in the field below her working on one last little sketch of the valley. She ran down and stood behind him, looking over his shoulder.

"Oh good, you've put in the Stoppel house," she said.

"Oh—and you've even got a bit of Ringelblume's stall!"

"That reminds me," said Daddy, adding a touch of gray to the cow-stall roof, "Ringelblume is going to have a very important afternoon."

"Important? Why, what's going to happen to her?" demanded Lucinda. "Something nice I hope?"

"Two things are going to happen to her, both extremely nice."

"What are they?" urged Lucinda impatiently.

"Well, she is to be taken out into the meadow with her mother this afternoon for her first visit to the great world beyond the stall. That is one thing. And the other I think you might guess. You've had a big share in it yourself."

"I know! It's her bell. She's going to wear her bell—is that it?" cried Lucinda, hopping up and down with excitement.

Daddy nodded.

"Annali found a little collar to fit her," he said. "She found it hanging on a nail behind the—" But before he could finish the sentence Lucinda was half-way down the field, flying in search of Annali to see the collar for herself.

Right after lunch they all trooped around to the cowstall. Annali brought the collar with its little tinkling bell and fastened it gently around Ringelblume's neck. At first the little calf rolled her large eyes anxiously, not at all sure she was going to like this strange thing on her neck. Then she tossed her head and the little bell rang softly, and as though bewitched by magic, Ringelblume calmed down.

84

"That's because she knows the sound of it," thought Lucinda, "and she knows it's her very own."

They led her out into the meadow then, and there she became a fairy calf indeed, flinging up her little brown heels and dancing among the daisies to the accompaniment of her bell. The children laughed and climbed the fence to watch her. But they soon tired of sitting still and drifted away to do something else, until only Lucinda remained on the fence, lost in some dream of her own. She would like to have stayed there for ever by herself, dreaming in the sunshine while the calf frisked among the flowers under the friendly mountain.

But somehow the afternoon slipped away and she was called in for one last meal on the balcony. But today she wasn't hungry and she soon begged to be allowed to go down and find the others.

She ran to the kitchen in search of the little girls. But the one she found was Johann, dressed in such magnificent clothes that she could only stand and stare. He wore a scarlet shirt under a short gray jacket, black trousers, and white patterned stockings, and around his waist the widest belt she had ever seen, patterned with edelweiss flowers. But the most spectacular part of it all was his hat, which was wide-brimmed and black, with a high narrow crown like Tante Anna's. But where hers had had only a tassel in front, his had two slender white feathers curling back from such a bunch of brilliant flowers that she wondered if he had picked a bloom from every one of her fifteen flowerpots, to get so many different colors. He had a flute in his hand and as she opened the door he was practicing an impressive-sounding trill.

Lucinda dashed to the bottom of the stairs and called up urgently, "Daddy, Daddy! Please come down and explain what's happened to Johann—he's dressed like a fairy-tale prince!"

Daddy and Mommy came hurrying down, just as Annali and Gretchen came into the room, beaming with sisterly pride.

"Ah, if only I had time to paint him now!" sighed Mommy, walking around to view him from every side, while Daddy asked questions in German.

"Well, it appears that Johann is a member of the village band," he explained at last, "and they're giving a concert down by the bridge this evening."

"Oh, may I go and hear them?" begged Lucinda. "Will there be time before the train leaves?"

Daddy talked it over in German with Annali.

"I don't see why you shouldn't go," he said. "Annali promises faithfully to bring you to the station in plenty of time. Don't forget to say good-by to Frau Stoppel before you go."

"And there's Ringelblume, too," Lucinda reminded him, making for the door.

She found the little calf lying asleep in a corner of the

meadow, tired out by all the excitement of the afternoon. But when Lucinda called out a quiet, "Good-by," she stirred in her sleep and a dreamy farewell tinkle sounded among the daisies.

Johann hurried on ahead while Lucinda said good-by to Frau Stoppel and Lisbet, and Daddy reminded Annali about the time of the train. It was already getting dusk when the children left the house and hurried toward the bridge. Lucinda soon began to run and Annali and Gretchen followed close on her heels, dragging Ludwig along between them.

The band was already assembling when they arrived and Lucinda was proud to feel that she actually knew one of the members. They were all as splendidly dressed as Johann and their shining instruments gleamed in the fading light. Someone distributed candles among the crowd and they lit them one from another.

Then the band struck up and away they marched in a blare of trumpets and drums, feathers waving in flower-decked hats and the candles softly flickering in the still evening air.

"It's just like a Christmas tree come to life!" thought Lucinda, as she was swept into the crowd with the others. They marched down the street to the square by the church, where they drew up under the trees, and there they stood in the candlelight while the band played on and on. It was all so strange and beautiful that Lucinda wondered if it was really a dream, and she stood in a trance of happiness clutching her candle in her hand, while the grease dripped onto her shoes.

Somehow she got to the station and into the little train with her parents, where she stood looking down through the open window at Annali, Gretchen, and Ludwig, whose candles were still alight.

There was a last-minute commotion, and there was dear Grossvater in his best suit, hurrying along the platform.

"A present to remind you of the woodcutter's hut in the woods," he said, holding something up to the window.

Annali raised her candle and Lucinda saw Saint Notburga. A perfectly carved little miniature of the figure on Grossvater's pump stood on his hand in the darkness, with the golden light from the candle shining on her hair!

"For me?" exclaimed Lucinda, sure she was dreaming now. "Oh, Grossvater, I'd rather have her than anything else in Tirol!"

The little toy train whistled shrilly and they were off. Annali and Gretchen waved their candles, and as the train chuffed into the darkness, the engine whistled again and the echo ran 'round the hills.

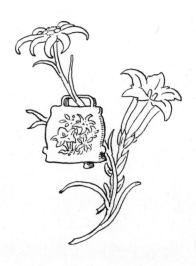